Christmas Tree Wood

Hardwick House

Four-Leaf Clover Field

River Noodle

Little Red

Dearest MDB—You guide me on my path, day by day,
and with you by my side I can follow my dreams.
Thank you for putting the magic back into my life.
—S. F.

For Sarah and Alfred.
Lifting spirits and sharing dreams.
—S. W.

SIMON & SCHUSTER
BOOKS FOR YOUNG READERS
An imprint of Simon & Schuster
Children's Publishing Division
1230 Avenue of the Americas,
New York, New York 10020
Text copyright © 2004 by Sarah,
The Duchess of York
Illustrations copyright © 2004 by Sam Williams
All rights reserved, including the right of
reproduction in whole or in part in any form.
SIMON & SCHUSTER BOOKS FOR YOUNG READERS
is a trademark of Simon & Schuster, Inc.
LITTLE RED is a trademark of Sarah, The
Duchess of York, and is used under license.
Book design by David Bennett
The text for this book is set in Goudy.
The illustrations for this book are rendered in soft
pencil and watercolor on Arches paper.

Manufactured in the United States of America
10 9 8 7 6 5 4 3 2 1
Library of Congress Cataloging-in-Publication
Data
York, Sarah Ferguson, Duchess of, 1959-
Little Red's Christmas Story / Sarah Ferguson,
the Duchess of York ; illustrated by Sam
Williams.— 1st ed.
p. cm.
Summary: Little Red's Christmas adventures
include a ride in Santa Claus' sleigh.
ISBN 0-689-85561-3 (hardcover)
[1. Dolls—Fiction. 2. Santa Claus—Fiction.
3. Friendship—Fiction. 4. Christmas—Fiction.]
I. Williams, Sam, 1955- ill. II. Title.
PZ7.Y823Li 2004
[E]—dc22
2003024413

Little Red's
Christmas Story

Sarah Ferguson
The Duchess of York

Illustrated by

Sam Williams

Simon & Schuster Books for Young Readers
New York   London   Toronto   Sydney

It was Christmas Eve at Buttercup Cottage. The house was covered with snow, and long squiggly icicles dangled from the roof. Little Red and her friends were ready to set off for Christmas Tree Wood, where their favorite little fir tree grew.

"Let's get a wiggle on!" said Little Red. "It's time to go, and we've got lots of presents to deliver along the way."

Singing carols, the merry gang crunched through the snow while snowflakes bustled all around.

They stopped at Purdey's Pasture to give the mouse family some sugary cinnamon sticks.

Then they headed for Sansome's Meadow. Little Red had made some delicious treacle shortbread for the robins who lived there.

And their last stop was to call on the badgers in Four-Leaf Clover Field. "I made this acorn necklace for you, Mrs. Badger," said Little Red proudly.

"And here's some of your favorite walnut fudge, Mr. Badger." She held out a beautifully wrapped bundle.

"Mmmm, thank you," said Mr. Badger. "Now, where are you off to next?"

"We're going to find our tree, yippee!" yelled Little Blue with glee.

The four friends arrived at the edge of Christmas Tree Wood.

"Yippeedoodledan!" cried Little Blue, hopping from foot to foot and getting tangled in his scarf. He had just started to build an enormous snowman, when Roany gave a cough.

"Ahem!" she snorted as carrots spluttered from her mouth. "I hate to break up the seasonal silliness, but what's that light coming from behind the trees?"

"Whatever can it be?" wondered Little Blue.

"I think I know who it could be," laughed Little Red merrily as she skipped through the wood.

There, in a clearing, stood Santa Claus with his sleigh and his eight reindeer.

"How lovely to see you!" said Little Red.

"By jingle, by jolly, by jove!" chortled Santa Claus. "If it's not my dear friend Little Red."

Little Blue, Roany, and Gino all looked on in amazement. They had no idea that Little Red was one of Santa Claus's friends!

"I am in a bit of a tizzy, my dear," explained Santa Claus. "Poor Percy has a bad cold, and he just can't go on any longer. I'll never be able to get all these presents delivered with only seven reindeer."

"I have an idea," said Little Red, looking gingerly at Roany.

"Oh, no!" said Roany, flicking her mane defiantly. "I'm sorry, but I can't fly and I won't fly."

As quick as a flash Little Red grabbed her sack of smiles, and before Roany could say "Jingle bells," she sprinkled magic flying dust all over the stubborn pony's hooves.

"Now you'll be able to fly!" announced Little Red triumphantly.

"We'll see about that," said a rather huffy Roany. "But even if you're right, I'll expect an enormous bunch of carrots and a mountain of sugar lumps."

"Your problem's solved, Santa Claus." Little Red giggled as she kissed Roany's velvety nose. "I know I can count on you," she whispered.

"Ho, ho, ho!" laughed Santa Claus. "But time's running out and I'm still going to need some extra help. Could you come too, Little Red?"

"I think so," she answered.

Then she turned to Little Blue. "I know that Percy will be safe in your care . . . and Bear, too," said Little Red as she handed her beloved teddy to her friend. "He doesn't like heights, you see."

Little Red clambered up to take her place next to Santa Claus on the sleigh. "I promise to bring you back a present, Little Blue!" she called.

"Eyes forward!" whooped Santa Claus to the reindeer and Roany as the sleigh whizzed off into the night air.

As Roany's hooves left the ground, the carrot she was chewing dropped from her open mouth. "Christmas crackers!" she gasped. "I'm flying!"

A very downcast Little Blue, with a snuffly Percy and a grumpy Gino, waved a sad good-bye to Little Red. How Little Blue would have loved to fly on Santa's sleigh! "I suppose we'd better go home," he sighed. "Gino, can you dig up our favorite tree to take back to Buttercup Cottage?" Gino threw Little Blue a disgruntled look as he dug the little tree out of the ground.

Little Blue loaded it onto the sled, popping Bear on top. He struggled to lead Percy with one hand and pull the sled with the other as they headed for home.

"Whoopee! Whizzing, whirling walnuts!" shrieked Little Red as the sleigh hurtled through the skies. But then a worried frown appeared on her forehead. "I do hope that Percy's feeling better, that Bear's all right, and that Little Blue remembers to hug them both," she said.

"There, there, don't despair. Your bear's in good care!" sang Santa Claus as they flew over the snowy rooftops.

It was late when Little Blue, Gino, and Percy trudged up the path to Buttercup Cottage. They were all tired, cold, and utterly fed up.

"Little Red has all the fun. I bet she forgets my present," muttered Little Blue as he dragged the fir tree through the front door. Curled up cosily in the armchair was Purdey. She bustled around, settling Percy by the fire and wrapping him in a blanket.

Then she brought him a hot-water bottle and carefully placed his hooves into a bucket of heated honeysuckle water.

Suddenly Little Blue's hair stood on end. "Dingly, dangly disasters and dog-eared doughnuts!" he cried. "Where's Bear?" Little Blue ran round and round in circles, getting more and more tangled in his scarf.

"He must have fallen off the sled! Little Red will never forgive me," he shrieked. "I've got to find him." And with that, Little Blue tore out of the cottage.

He stumbled in the direction of Christmas Tree Wood, with tears streaming down his face. "I'm a hopeless friend," he whimpered. "I'm not just Little Blue, I'm very blue."

But just as he turned the corner into Sansome's Meadow, he met Mrs. Badger trundling her wheelbarrow full of little badgers. Through his tears Little Blue noticed a small paw waving from the wheelbarrow. It wasn't a badger paw . . . it was Bear's paw!

"Oh, oh, oh, Mrs. Badger, you've found Bear!" he cried, hugging and squeezing her with all his might.

"Yes, dear," said Mrs. Badger. "I found him half-buried in the snow outside our house and recognized him straightaway. I know how fond Little Red is of her bear so I thought I should return him, quick sticks!"

"Christmaspuddingtastic!" laughed Little Blue, and he wrapped Bear very carefully in his scarf. Then he told Mrs. Badger all about Little Red's adventure. "Why don't you come back to Buttercup Cottage with me—you could help me decorate the tree. I'm all behind like Roany's tail, and we must finish before Little Red and Roany get back."

So, with Mrs. Badger and all the baby badgers and with Bear tucked inside his scarf, Little Blue rushed back to Buttercup Cottage.

Everyone helped to decorate the Christmas tree . . . and the cottage . . . and even Percy's antlers. As they worked, they slurped marshmallow cocoa and crunched on crusty custard Christmas crumpets.

Suddenly Gino began barking excitedly and ran to the window. "Someone must be outside," said Little Blue as he undid the latch and opened the door, just as . . .

Little Red walked down the path, laden with presents. Roany was smirking smugly from ear to ear.

Little Red hugged and kissed each of her friends in turn. Then everyone looked to the sky and waved to Santa as his sleigh flew up into the stars.

"Thank you for a wonderful adventure, Santa Claus. We'll send Percy back to you when he's quite, quite better," called Little Red.

"Come inside, Little Red. You must be frozen," fussed Mrs. Badger. "Yes, do hurry, Little Red," said Little Blue as he eagerly eyed the pile of presents. Everyone followed him into Buttercup Cottage as he pulled Little Red by the sleeve.

"How Christmasy everything looks! The tree is just beautiful!" gasped Little Red, hugging Bear close to her heart. "Little Blue," she said, handing him a very odd-shaped parcel, "this is for you. Thank you so much for looking after Percy and Bear. What a true friend you are!"

"A horn!" cried Little Blue. "Fantabuloso! Toot, toot! It's just the thing to make my tricycle go faster!"

"Ahem," sniffed Roany. "And what about my present?"

"Oh, Roany, you've been the biggest star in the universe!" said Little Red. "That's why Santa Claus wanted you to have these as an extra-special treat."

Roany's eyes sparkled as Little Red placed a bucket full of crunchy, candy-coated Christmas carrots in front of her. "It was a piece of Christmas carrot cake!" Roany chuckled.

Little Red raised her cup of marshmallow cocoa.
"Hurray for Little Blue, and hurray for Roany!" she
laughed proudly.

"Hip hip hooray, we've all saved Christmas Day!"
everyone cheered.

The Village

Sansome's
Meadow

Buttercup Cottage

Purdey's Pasture

Lily Pad Pond